SCHOLASTIC

Let's Find Out

My REBUS Reader

I0890031

I Put On My Shoes

by Pamela Chanko

SCHOLASTIC INC.

New York Toronto London Auckland Sydney New Delhi Hong Kong

I put **brown** shoes on my  .

feet

I put **pink** shoes on my 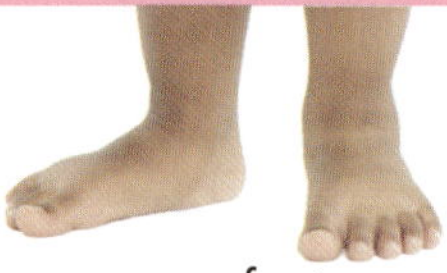 .

feet

I put **red** shoes on my 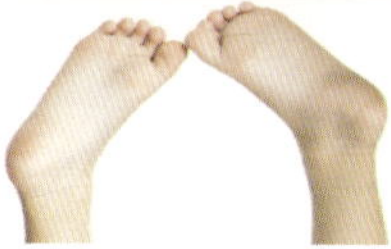 .

feet

I put **yellow** shoes on my 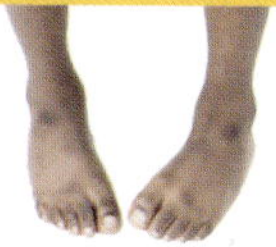 .

feet

I put **blue** shoes on my 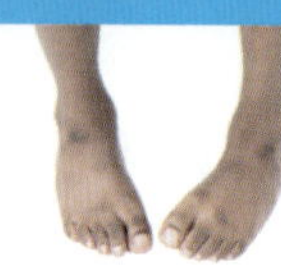 .

feet

I put **black** shoes on my 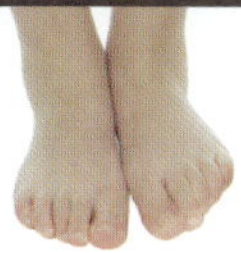 feet .

I put **green** shoes on my 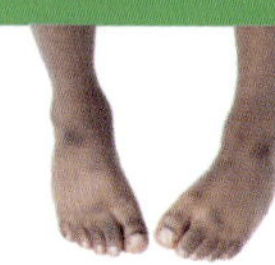 .

feet